Snake
on the bus
and other pet stories

Also edited by Valerie Bierman

Best of Friends
No More School
Streets Ahead

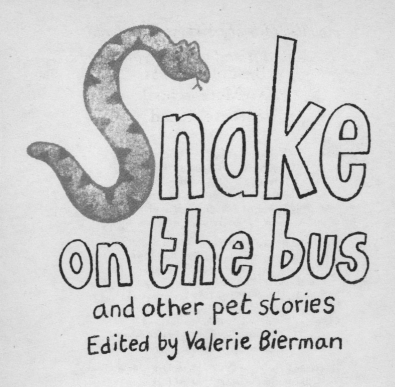

Snake on the bus

and other pet stories

Edited by Valerie Bierman

Illustrated by Nick Sharratt

MAMMOTH

Remembering Robert Westall, who loved cats. A good friend and a great writer.

First published in Great Britain 1994
by Methuen Children's Books
Published 1995 by Mammoth
an imprint of Reed International Books Limited
Michelin House, 81 Fulham Road, London SW3 6RB
and Auckland, Melbourne, Singapore and Toronto

'You Can't Bring That in Here' © 1994 Robert Swindells
'Snake on the Bus' © 1994 Hazel Townson
'Mairi's Mermaid' © 1994 Michael Morpurgo
'Wind-Cat' © 1994 The Estate of Robert Westall
'Jekyll and Jane' © 1994 Terrance Dicks
'Everton' © 1994 Jacqueline Wilson
'Pitchou' © 1994 Jamila Gavin
'The Ghost Gorilla' © 1994 Chris Powling
'Hair of a Cat' © 1994 Pat Thomson

This volume copyright © 1994 Methuen Children's Books
Illustrations copyright © 1994 Nick Sharratt

The authors have asserted their moral rights in accordance
with the Copyright, Designs and Patents Act 1988

ISBN 0 7497 2389 0

A CIP catalogue record for this title
is available from the British Library

Printed and bound in Great Britain
by Cox & Wyman Ltd, Reading, Berkshire

Contents

Foreword   7
  Valerie Bierman

You Can't Bring That in Here   9
  Robert Swindells

Snake on the Bus   18
  Hazel Townson

Mairi's Mermaid   25
  Michael Morpurgo

Wind-Cat   34
  Robert Westall

Jekyll and Jane   37
  Terrance Dicks

Everton   49
  Jacqueline Wilson

Pitchou   59
  Jamila Gavin

The Ghost Gorilla   76
  Chris Powling

Hair of a Cat   87
  Pat Thomson

Foreword

These stories are for anyone who has ever loved a pet – whether real or imaginary. I have always had a cat in my life, from the sleek black cat I had when I was small to our present two – Jo, large, fat, black and white, and Minnie, dainty, timid, ginger and white. There is a long way to go to catch up with the sixty seven cats cared for by Robert Westall during his lifetime! You can read the poem written one windy night when watching his cat Jeoffrey chasing *The Wind Cat*. And there are a further eight stories about pets – some very much alive, like Everton the cat or Jane the dog, but there is also a mermaid and a ghostly gorilla! All shapes and sizes, large and small, timid or fierce – there are all kinds of pets to suit all kinds of people. I hope you find a story here to suit YOU!

Robert Swindells

YOU CAN'T BRING THAT IN HERE

Jimmy was absolutely fed up. His mum and dad had gone off to work in America for two years, leaving him to be looked after by his grown-up brother, Osbert. Looked after! That was a laugh, for a start. Osbert had worked in a bakery, but as soon as Mum and Dad started sending money from America, he chucked his job. Nowadays he spent most of his time lying on the sofa in his vest watching telly, slurping beer straight from the can and making rude

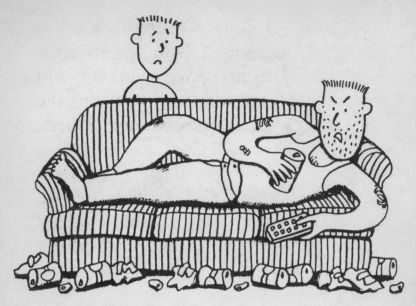

noises. He neither washed nor shaved nor did anything around the house. The place smelled awful, and the sofa looked like a tatty boat afloat on a sea of can rings, beercans and screwed-up crisp packets.

Jimmy had to go to school, and when school was over he never had any fun. He couldn't bring his friends home because they were all scared of Osbert, and if there was something good on telly his brother always said, 'Shove off, kid – I'm watching *this*.'

He made Jimmy do all the work — shopping, cooking, cleaning, ironing, gardening — in his spare time. On cold mornings Jimmy had to sit on the lavatory to warm the seat for Osbert, and at bedtime he had to lie in his brother's freezing bed till the sheets were warmed and Osbert came to kick him out. Soon his friends stopped bothering with him, because he couldn't play out or go to football. He grew lonely and sad.

One day on his way home from school, Jimmy found a baby bird which had fallen out of its nest. It was fluffy and cute and Jimmy felt sorry for it. 'It's all right, little bird,' he murmured. 'I'm going to take you home and look after you.'

But when he got home Osbert said, 'You can't bring that in here.'

'Why not?' asked Jimmy, dismayed.

'Birds make a mess,' said Osbert, brushing crumbs off his vest.

'Take it away. Get rid of it.'

11

Jimmy sniffled as he walked along the street with the nestling cupped in his hands. How could he get rid of it? If he put it down, a cat would get it.

He met an old lady. 'What have you got there?' she asked. Jimmy showed her. 'Oh, the poor wee creature,' she said. 'And are you its new mammy?' Jimmy told the old lady about Osbert and she said, 'I'll tell you what we'll do. I have a beautiful kitten at home. I'll swap you – your bird for my kitten.'

Jimmy was sure Osbert would fall for

the kitten, but he didn't. 'You can't bring that in here,' he said.

'Why not?' asked Jimmy.

'Kittens make a mess,' said Osbert, throwing an empty can across the room. 'Get it out.'

Jimmy put the kitten in his pocket and went out. 'Maybe I should take you back to the old lady,' he whispered, but just then a boy from his school came along.

'Hi, Jimmy,' he said. 'What's that in your pocket?' Jimmy showed him the kitten and told him about Osbert. 'I know,' said the boy. 'I'll take the kitten, and you can have my gerbil.'

'You can't bring that in here,' growled Osbert from the sofa. 'Gerbils throw their food around.'

'But – but . . .' stammered Jimmy.

'No buts!' roared Osbert, chucking half a pork pie at Jimmy's head. 'Get it out of here.'

Jimmy put the gerbil in his pocket and went out. It was getting dark and he was hungry. An old man was coming along the street with a puppy on a lead. 'What's up, son?' he asked, because Jimmy was crying a bit. He told the old man about the gerbil, and about Osbert. 'Well, here,' said the old man. 'Give me your gerbil and take my puppy. Nobody can resist a puppy.'

Osbert could resist a puppy. 'You can't bring that in here,' he snarled. 'Puppies wreck the place.'

'Yes, but . . .' murmured Jimmy.

'No buts!' screamed Osbert, pounding the sofa with his fist till the arm fell off. 'Get it out of here, and when you come back you can get my tea – I'm starving.'

Jimmy was starving too, but he couldn't just abandon the puppy. He trailed along the street holding the lead, wondering what to do. I could try the R.S.P.C.A., he thought. They'd look after him. But when he got to the R.S.P.C.A. it was shut. He was standing, looking at the CLOSED sign and wondering what to do, when a van drew up and a man got out. 'Oh, heck,' the man sighed. 'Closed, and I thought I'd be getting rid of him at last.'

'Who?' asked Jimmy.

'My pet,' growled the man. 'That's who.'

'Why d'you want rid of him?' Jimmy asked.

' 'Cause he's a gorilla,' said the man.

'A gorilla?' Jimmy was amazed.

The man nodded. 'Aye. Cute and cuddly he was, when he was small, but now . . .' He led Jimmy to the back of the van. 'Look.'

Jimmy peered through the window. Inside the van sat an enormous gorilla. 'Wow!' he gasped. 'What does he eat?'

'Bananas,' said the man. 'Loads and loads of bananas.'

'And where does he sleep?'

'In my bed,' said the man. 'He kicked me out six months ago and now I have to make do with the floor.'

'I'll swap you,' offered Jimmy. 'My puppy for your gorilla.'

The man shook his head. 'You don't want a gorilla, son,' he said.

'Oh yes I do!' cried Jimmy.

Osbert was still on the sofa when Jimmy walked in, his fist buried in the gorilla's giant paw. It was dark in the room and Osbert couldn't see his brother's new pet clearly. 'You can't bring that in here,' he said.

'He isn't bringing me,' rumbled the gorilla. 'I'm bringing *him*. And you can get off that sofa – it's mine.'

Everything's changed at Jimmy's house now. The place sparkles, which isn't surprising because Osbert never stops cleaning it. He daren't stop, because Bozo the gorilla likes a tidy house, and Bozo usually gets what he wants. When Osbert isn't lugging great bagfuls of bananas from the supermarket he's sweeping, polishing, dusting and hoovering. Jimmy's friends drop in all the time to watch TV, play video games and see Bozo. Until recently Osbert had a girlfriend, but she's left him now. She didn't like it when Osbert brought her home one evening and Bozo said, 'You can't bring that in here.'

Hazel Townson

SNAKE ON THE BUS

It was Barney's birthday, though he still had to go to school. He opened his presents and cards at breakfast and collected quite a lot of money as well as some interesting parcels.

'One more present still to come,' said Dad mysteriously. 'You can have it tonight.'

Barney took his birthday money to school and spent it on a snake; a real, live snake.

Well, his parents had said he could

buy what he wanted with the money, and he'd had his eye on this snake for weeks in the window of the pet shop next door to school. Its name was Sneaky. Now Sneaky was curled in a box on Barney's lap on the back seat of the school bus, going home. Would there be trouble when they arrived? Barney hoped not, but he could not help feeling just a little bit worried, all the same.

On the seat next to Barney his friend Nina was having her hair pulled by Mike the bully. Mike was leaning over from the seat in front, dragging Nina's head towards him.

'Ow! That hurts!' yelled Nina, who was only half the size of Mike.

'Give us your chocolate and I'll stop,' said Mike.

'Never!' screeched Nina. She had bought the chocolate for her brother, who was laid up at home with a broken leg.

'We'll see about that!' shouted Mike, pulling so hard that he dragged Nina

right off the seat. There was a crash and a cry, followed by a scuffle as Mike leapt from his seat and tried to snatch the chocolate from Nina's hand.

Barney wasn't having that! He jumped up, eager to help his friend. But in his excitement he forgot about Sneaky. The cardboard box slid off Barney's lap, the lid flew off the box and Sneaky slithered out, making straight for Mike's ankles.

'Help! A snake!' Mike hollered, fleeing

down the aisle.

'What's going on back there?' yelled Tom, the school bus driver. 'Any trouble and you'll all be sorry!'

Tom had been driving the school bus for years, and did not intend to put up with any nonsense.

'There's a snake on the bus, honest!' Mike went on. 'It's after me! It's just gone under that seat.'

Most of the children knew about Barney's snake, for he had let them peep into the box at the bus stop. But none of them liked Mike the bully, so they all kept Barney's secret to themselves.

'I can't see any snake, can you?' they asked one another.

'He's making it up to frighten us.'

'Just the sort of thing he *would* do!'

'Don't take any notice of him, Tom!'

They were so convincing that even Mike began to wonder if he had imagined the snake. He sat down again, keeping a wary eye on the bus floor all the same.

Mike lived nearest to school so he was always first to get off the bus. Today he was glad when the bus reached his stop. He flew to the door, leapt down the steps and bolted along the pavement as fast as he could go. He did not notice that Sneaky had also made a quick exit from the bus and had slithered through the gateway of a much overgrown and tangled garden.

The children in the front seats noticed, though. They began to shout to Tom to wait a minute because the snake had escaped.

'You just said there *was* no snake!' Tom retorted crossly as he drove off. 'I don't know what you kids are up to, but the next one to mention a snake gets reported to the Head teacher tomorrow.'

Barney was really upset. He ran down the aisle, wanting to get off the bus to go and look for Sneaky, but Tom would not let him.

'I'm responsible for seeing you safe

home,' said Tom, ordering Barney back to his seat.

It was a desolate homecoming, not a bit like a birthday. Barney walked in with his empty box.

'What's that?' asked his mother, and the whole sad story came tumbling out. It no longer mattered whether his parents would *mind* having a snake, as there was not going to be one after all.

To Barney's hurt surprise, instead of consoling him his mother began to smile. But he soon found out why, for when Dad came home a little while later he was carrying a huge tank containing – a snake!

'Your belated birthday present,' grinned Dad. 'We knew you wanted a snake, but I couldn't collect it until this afternoon.'

Great! Barney could not help being pleased. 'But what about Sneaky?'

'Jump in the car and show me the garden where your friends said Sneaky had gone,' Dad decided.

They drove to the garden at once – and there Sneaky was, curled up sleepily in the long grass. Dad had a word with the owners of the house, who were only too glad to let him take Sneaky away. Barney put Sneaky back into his box, which he had brought with him hopefully, and they drove back home.

'Now you've got a playmate as well,' Barney told his pet. 'Just wait till Mike the bully hears about that!'

Michael Morpurgo

MAIRI'S MERMAID

Mairi still could not swim. She wished
she could, but she just couldn't. All the
holidays she'd been trying, but every
time she took her feet off the bottom she
sank like a stone and swallowed
mouthfuls of salty seawater. Her
brother, Robbie, swam like a fish. 'It's
easy,' he told her. 'You believe in
mermaids, don't you? Well, you just
pretend you're a mermaid, like this.' He
squawked with laughter and plunged
headfirst into another towering green

wave. He could be very annoying at times.

Her mother and father tried to help. 'It'll come,' they said. 'You'll do it.' But it didn't come and she didn't do it. 'Come and build sandcastles with us, instead,' they said. But Mairi wanted to be miserable all on her own. She spent the rest of the holidays at the other end of the beach, the rocky end, pottering in amongst the rock pools looking for crabs and trying to forget all about swimming.

It was the last morning of the holidays and Mairi had already collected five little green crabs in her bucket. They'd be her pets for the day. Later, just before they left the beach, she'd let them go and watch them sidle away into the sea. She just wanted one or two more, so she wandered over towards the rock pool nearest the sea. She'd even found a lobster in there once.

She sat on the edge of the rock pool, dangling her feet in the weeds at the bottom. The water was warm from the sun. She bent over and soon found two little crabs scuttling around. She caught them and dropped them into her bucket. There was a starfish, several sea-anemones and a shoal of silver fish darting around her legs. Swimming looked so easy for them, she thought.

Something pinched her toe. She thought it might be a crab and jumped up. It was nothing. Maybe she had imagined it. But just to be sure, she decided she wasn't going to dangle her feet again. She lay on her stomach and felt in amongst the weed for more crabs. Something tugged her finger; once, twice. And then she heard a piping voice. It seemed at first to come from far away. She listened again. It came from deep down in the rock pool. Mairi brushed aside the seaweed, and there was a huge brown crab glaring up at her and in his great grasping claw was a fish no bigger than her finger. But then she saw it wasn't a fish, not an ordinary fish

anyway. It was a fish with arms and hands, a fish with a head like her own and hair, and a mouth that spoke. It was a little mermaid.

'Help!' cried the mermaid. 'Help me!' Mairi was not at all afraid of crabs, however big they were. She picked the crab out of the water and shook him and shook him until the little mermaid dropped into the pool and disappeared. Mairi put the crab in her bucket. It was the biggest she'd ever found.

For a moment or two there was no sign of the little mermaid. Then a small head bobbed up. 'Thank you, oh, thank you,' said the mermaid.

Mairi never knew mermaids could be this small. She wasn't sure mermaids were even real. 'Are you real?' she said.

'Course I'm real,' piped the mermaid. 'You've got to help me, please. I must find my mother. She'll be worried sick. I went off on my own and I got stuck in this pool and then that great big horrible crab caught me and if you hadn't come he'd have eaten me right up. Take me back to the sea, take me back to my mother, please, please, *please*!'

Mairi would so like to have kept her as a pet for a day. She'd love to have seen Robbie's face – he never even believed in mermaids – but she knew what she had to do. She dipped her cupped hands into the pool and scooped the little mermaid out. She climbed carefully over the limpet-covered rocks down to the sea. Then she crouched down, opened her hands, and let the mermaid go. But the mermaid wouldn't go.

'No, no!' cried the little mermaid clutching her thumb. 'Not here. The waves will smash me against the rocks. Take me further out, please, out to that rock over there. That's where we all live, in a big cave under that rock.'

'But I can't swim,' said Mairi.

'Course you can,' replied the little mermaid. 'Anyone can. It's easy. Please, it's not far.'

'I'll tell you what,' Mairi said. 'I'll take you as far as I can walk, but I can't go out of my depth.' And she stepped into the sea and waded out until the sea water came as high as her knees, as high as her waist, as high as her neck. Suddenly a giant wave came rolling in and lifted her right off her feet. When she came down there was no sandy bottom under her feet, no bottom at all. Mairi kicked and splashed and the seawater came into her mouth.

'It's all right,' said the little mermaid. 'You're swimming! You're swimming!'

And when Mairi kicked again, she did not sink. She was swimming, she was! She lifted her chin and paddled through the sea, keeping her mouth tight closed.

'See? It's easy, isn't it?' piped the little mermaid. And together they swam out towards the rock.

They were almost there when Mairi felt an arm around her waist, then another and another. The sea around her was suddenly full of mermaids. 'She saved me, Mother,' cried the little mermaid, clinging to her mother's hair. 'She saved me.'

Then Mairi felt the rock beneath her feet and could stand, the sea breaking around her legs. The little mermaid was telling everyone her story. 'And look what the crab did to my tail,' she said.

'Maybe it'll teach you not to go off like that,' said her mother. 'I've told you and told you. If it hadn't have been for this girl – well, it doesn't bear thinking about.' She smiled at Mairi. 'How can we ever thank you enough?' she said. And Mairi had a sudden idea.

'You couldn't teach me how to swim, could you?' she asked. 'I mean, like you do, like mermaids do.'

Some time later Robbie was waiting for the next really big wave to come curling in, waiting for just the right one to dive into. 'Look at this one!' he cried, as a great green wave came curling in. He was about to dive into it when he saw what looked like a seal swimming along the crest of the wave. But it wasn't a seal, it was Mairi. It was Mairi swimming! As she swept past him, his mouth opened in astonishment and the seawater went in.

'You can swim!' he spluttered.

Mairi's mother and father came running down to the water's edge. 'You can swim!' they cried.

'Course I can,' she said. 'It's easy. I just pretended I was a mermaid.'

Robert Westall

WIND-CAT

Jeoffrey will not go out tonight,
Hovers by the cat-flap, paw uplifted,
Eyes wide and wild ears pricked
Listening to wind-cat prowling the earth.

Wind-cat assaults the cat-flap violently
With invisible paws,
But does not come in,
Does not have a smell,
But spits savagely in Jeoffrey's face,
Then retires to leap through the garden
Tearing and smashing fearsomely

At Jeoffrey's trees,
Making Jeoffrey's fence
Creak violently;
Transmitting his terrible size,
Then is back, rattling the flap,
Spitting again, a fearsome show.

Yet Jeoffrey
Is not entirely convinced.
How can so great a creature have no smell
But the usual grass, earth and trees?
Jeoffrey suspects a con
Until the cat next door,
The usual cat-flap burglar,
Terror of the road,
Streaks past the window
Cowering to the earth,
Soaked, blown and beaten
By the wind-cat's paws.

Jeoffrey seems to shrug,
Retires to the lounge
To wash, by the fire
And guard the house against
An infinitely smaller wind-cat
Burgling down the chimney.
He knows his limitations,
That's his strength.

Terrance Dicks

JEKYLL AND JANE

You know that old story about Dr Jekyll and Mr Hyde?

I've never actually read the book but I saw the film on telly. It's all about this kindly old Dr Jekyll who invents some kind of magic potion. Every time he takes it he turns into horrible Mr Hyde, and goes raving round the town doing horrible deeds.

Well, we've got a Jekyll and Hyde dog. Her name's Jane. She's a mongrel with a bit of beagle in her, a smallish black and brown animal with big floppy ears, and an amazing amount of energy. The one thing she really loves is her daily walk. Luckily we live very near the Common.

It was the walks that caused all the trouble.

When we'd finally persuaded Mum and Dad to let us have a dog we'd promised to take it for a walk every week-day after school.

But you know how it is when you stagger home from a hard day's school. All you fancy is a jam butty and a slump in front of the telly. A nice healthy walk is the last thing on your mind.

Sally and I started taking turns. Then one of us would say, 'You take her today and I'll take her the next two times.'

A complicated system of dog walk debts grew up and we often lost track of whose turn it really was, each insisting it was the other's go. One day we both refused to give in – and Jane didn't get her walk.

Next day at walk time Jane was

nowhere in sight. She'd been out in the garden – but she wasn't there now.

Sally and I panicked and dashed out to search the Common. We looked everywhere, running up to every black and brown dog in sight, but none of them were Jane.

We staggered back home exhausted – and found Jane waiting for us on the doorstep. We made a big fuss of her, and took her inside, promising we'd never let her miss her walk again.

And we didn't – for a time. Then we got lazy again, and Jane missed another walk.

Once again she disappeared. But this time I didn't panic. 'Look, she knows her way home,' I said. 'She'll come back when she's ready.'

Sure enough, about an hour later there came a barking at the front door. Jane was back.

'What we've got here is a self-walking dog,' I said. 'We might as well leave things to her.'

So that's what we did. At weekends the whole family took her for long walks. On weekdays Jane made her own arrangements, leaving us free to be couch potatoes. This went on so long that we took it for granted – though somehow we never got round to telling Mum and Dad.

One day Sally read something out from the local paper. *Mystery Dog Terrorises Common*. Apparently a number of dog walkers had complained that a huge savage dog had appeared

out of nowhere and set about their beloved pets.

'I was just taking my sheepdog Bertie for a walk,' said one lady. 'A giant dog leaped out of the bushes barking and growling. It was brown and black with big ears and glowing eyes.' Apparently she'd managed to drive the beast off with her umbrella.

Sally and I looked at each other – and at Jane who had just come back from her solo walk.

'It couldn't be . . .' said Sally.

'No, of course not,' I said. 'Jane's black and brown, but she's little and cute, not huge and savage. And she never gets into fights. It must be some stray dog that's gone wild. They'll catch it soon.'

But they didn't. The stories went on appearing, week after week and the mystery dog got bigger and fiercer with every story. It got into the national press and there was even a jokey item on at the end of the TV news. *Hound of the*

Baskervilles Returns. Mum and Dad watched it, and they both looked at Jane.

'You'd better be careful when you're out on the Common with Jane,' said Mum. 'You haven't seen this monster, have you?'

'Not a sign,' I said. 'I think they must be making it all up.' But they weren't.

One day Jane was late coming back from her walk. It was getting near the time Mum and Dad got home, and I was a bit worried. I went outside and stood on the front steps, looking down the road towards the Common wondering if I ought to go out and start searching. Suddenly I saw Jane trotting up the road towards me. I felt really relieved – but not for long.

We'd got a new neighbour next door but one, a large posh lady with a large posh poodle – one of those really big woolly ones. Its name was Fifi, it had one of those special poodle-parlour haircuts and it was her pride and joy.

As Jane came up the street the poodle and its owner came out of their house and started down the street towards her.

Suddenly Jane spotted Fifi – and the transformation began. All Jane's hair stood on end so that she really did look twice her usual size. Her lips drew back and she gave the sort of blood-curdling growl that you expect from a Doberman on a bad day. She streaked towards the poodle so fast that her ears flattened back in the slipstream.

I hurtled down the steps to intercept her. Our neighbour had stopped to chat with someone and was unaware of the monster speeding towards them. Just as Jane reached her target I grabbed her by the collar and yanked her back. I was nearly in time – but not quite. As I hauled Jane away she had a clump of woolly poodle-fur between her teeth.

There was a terrible fuss after that. Jane was growling, Fifi was howling and her owner was screaming at me.

I gave Jane a good shake and yelled, 'Stop it!' You could actually see sanity return. Her fur flattened, and her head, tail and ears dropped down.

'Is that dog yours?' snapped Fifi's owner.

I was tempted to deny it – but at that moment Jane pulled away from me and dashed up the steps and into our house.

'I should like to see your parents,' said the lady grimly.

'They're out,' I said, and bolted up the steps after Jane. Back in the house I told Sally what had happened.

'Oh no!' she gasped. 'Jane, how could you?'

Jane curled up in her basket and pretended to be asleep.

I still say what happened next wasn't really my fault. It was just bad luck. Mum came home, and I was just bracing myself to tell her the bad news when Dad got back as well, a few minutes after her as usual. He was just hanging up his coat when the doorbell rang. Jane ran to the front door and started barking.

'Good old Jane, what a watchdog,' said Dad, and went to open the front door.

'Dad, wait!' I yelled, but it was too late.

Now it was fair enough Fifi's owner coming to complain. But I still say it was silly of her to bring Fifi . . .

Dad opened the door, Jane at his heels – and Jane saw Fifi standing right on her doorstep!

It was the full Jekyll and Hyde all over again. Jane's fur swelled up, her lips drew back, she gave a bloodcurdling growl and she hurled herself on poor Fifi. Dad made a frantic grab at Jane's collar and pulled her back – with another chunk of poodle fur between her teeth!

Fifi's owner went into a state of total hysteria.

I must say Dad coped surprisingly well. He yelled at Jane so loudly she dived straight into her basket and didn't move for another hour. He and Mum talked themselves hoarse calming down our new neighbour, swearing that Jane must have had a touch of temporary insanity, and that she would never again be allowed anywhere near Fifi. They sympathised with Fifi's shattered nerves and promised to pay for a complete new hairdo at the poodle beauty parlour.

When they'd finally got rid of Fifi and her owner they came back into the kitchen and Mum said, 'Well?'

Sally and I made a full confession. When we'd finished Dad said, 'Right.

Come on, you two!'

He stomped out to the car and Sally and I followed. I wasn't sure if we were being driven to the police station or the orphanage, but it turned out to be the local DIY centre.

We loaded up with wire and trellis-work, drove back home, and we all helped Dad transform the back garden into a fair imitation of a maximum security prison.

'And you two had better see she doesn't get out the front way,' said Mum. 'We got off lightly this time!'

Jane's days of solitary freedom are over now. She gets plenty of walks but all with human company. We keep an eye out for other dogs as well. If it's a little dog, there's nothing to worry about. If it's a smooth-coated dog of any shape or size, everything's fine.

But if the approaching dog is both large and woolly, we grab Jane quick and put her back on her lead. As we drag her past, the hair on her neck rises, just a bit, and we hear a low rumbling growl. Somewhere inside our lovable little family pet, the Monster of the Common is lurking still.

These days we don't take any chances. . . .

Jacqueline Wilson

EVERTON

Mum said it was going to be all right.
Dad said it was going to be all right.
Laura said it was going to be all right.
But Danny wasn't so sure.

It was all happening so quickly. Last week all he had to worry about was swopping his Marmite sandwiches at lunchtime and Jacko Jackson and his gang maybe beating him up behind the bike sheds. Just the usual sort of school worries. Home was where you flopped on the floor in front of the telly or played your computer games up in your bedroom. Home was Mum, Dad, Laura and Everton and you just took them for granted.

But this week it had all changed. Mum told him and Danny had to keep shaking his head and wrinkling up his nose because he couldn't take it in. There wasn't going to be a home any more. Mum and Dad were splitting up. Dad was going off with some other lady. Mum was getting a new flat. Mum and Laura were already making plans about the furniture and the carpets and the curtains. Mum and Laura seemed to be best friends now, not just mother and daughter.

'What about me?' said Danny.

'You'll live in the flat with us, Danny. Don't worry. You can have your own bedroom with all your computer stuff,' said Mum.

'But I don't want a new bedroom in a new house,' said Danny. 'Why can't we stay here?'

Mum sighed. 'Danny, didn't you understand what we said? We're having to sell this house. But it's going to be all right, you'll see. You'll like the new flat, I promise you.'

But Mum didn't sound so sure now.

'It's going to be all right, Mum,' said Laura. 'We'll get on just fine, you and me and Danny.'

'What about Dad?' said Danny.

Mum looked as if she might cry. Laura looked furious.

'We don't want Dad,' said Laura.

'I do,' said Danny.

He loved his Dad, even though he had been away a lot recently. Dad and Danny played football in the back garden. Dad and Danny had wrestling matches. Dad and Danny told each other silly jokes and roared with laughter.

Danny wanted to laugh with Dad, not cry with Mum.

'I want to live with Dad!' said Danny.

He told Dad when he saw him.

'I want you to live with me too, Danny,' said Dad. 'But . . .'

As soon as Dad said 'but', Danny knew it was no use. Dad gave all sorts of explanations. His new flat wasn't big enough. He had to go away on work trips. So did his new lady. There wouldn't be anyone to look after Danny some nights.

'But you can still come and stay with us some weekends. We'd love that. You and Laura.'

'No fear,' said Laura, sniffing. She might be best friends with Mum now but she was worst enemies with Dad.

Danny felt as if he was worst enemies with everyone. His mouth felt sour, as if he'd had to eat a whole jar of Marmite. He felt sore all over, as if Jacko Jackson and his gang had been beating him up all day long.

He hunched in a corner and pulled Everton onto his lap for comfort. Danny had had Everton ever since he was a kitten. He wasn't an Everton football fan. He was named after Everton mints, which are black and white. Even Everton's face was black and white, black round one eye and white round the other. He wasn't a very pretty cat, but Danny thought he was perfect.

'*Purr*fect,' said Danny. It was an old joke. Only nothing seemed funny any more.

'What about Everton?' said Danny.

Mum looked worried. 'Oh dear. Yes. Everton,' she said.

'Everton won't like going to the new flat. Cats don't like moving,' said Danny.

'Mmm,' said Mum. 'So maybe it might be kinder if we asked around the neighbourhood to see if anyone wants to take him in?'

'What?' said Danny, outraged. 'Everton's *my* cat.'

'Yes, I know, Danny, but the new flat isn't really right for pets,' said Mum.

'It's not right for me, either!' Danny shouted. 'I'm going to stay here. With

Everton.'

Danny couldn't stay in the old house because it was sold. He had to go to the new flat with Mum and Laura. But Everton went too.

'All right. We'll take Everton with us. Don't worry, Danny.'

So they moved to the new flat, Mum and Laura and Danny and Everton. Mum still cried sometimes and Laura got very cross but they seemed to like the new flat even so. They had brand-new leather furniture and a pale grey carpet. Everton and Danny were always in trouble for scratching the sofa or trailing muddy footprints across the carpet.

'I must have been mad to say we'd keep that wretched cat,' Mum said, scooping Everton up and sending him yowling from the room. 'He's even been clawing at the new curtains, look!'

'He doesn't like it here,' said Danny. 'He wants to go home.'

'This is home now,' said Mum.

'Well, it doesn't feel like it,' said Danny.

He went off to his new bedroom in a sulk and played computer games. *Zap, zap, zap. Zap* went Mum. *Zap* went Dad. *Zap* went Laura. Danny and Everton rose to higher and higher levels, Boy Wonder and Clever Cat.

Danny looked round. Where had Everton got to? He went out of his bedroom and looked all around the flat. No Everton. Mum hadn't seen him. Neither had Laura. The kitchen window was open. It looked like Everton had escaped.

'He'll be back for his tea,' said Mum.

But he wasn't. Danny stood on the balcony, calling until he was hoarse. Then Laura went out to look in the street outside. It was a busy road. She was gone a while. Then she came back holding her cardigan in her arms. She was crying, and yet Laura didn't ever cry.

'No!' said Danny.

Everton was inside the cardigan. He'd been run over. He wasn't used to so much traffic.

'His tummy,' sobbed Laura.

'Quick. The vet,' said Mum.

They went in the car. Danny held Everton now. Everton usually hated car rides and struggled. He didn't struggle at all this time.

They got Everton to the vet but he wasn't so sure he could help. There was an operation he could try, but he didn't know if Everton would pull through. And then it would take weeks of careful nursing. . . .

'Let's try the operation. It's our only chance. And then we'll nurse him,' said Mum.

Danny held poor Everton in his arms.

'It's going to be all right, Everton,' Danny whispered, though he didn't believe it.

Everton had his operation. Danny cried, waiting to be told that Everton had died.

But he didn't die. He came through the operation. He stayed at the vet's for a couple of days. He could barely lift his head. He looked very ill. But he was still alive.

Mum collected him from the vet's. She stayed off work for a week to nurse him. Laura looked after him too. And Danny. Everton needed three people because he was in a bad way, especially when he was well enough to walk. He'd always been a clean cat, careful in his habits, but now he'd lost control. The new pale grey carpet kept getting horribly stained.

'I'm sorry, Mum,' said Danny, getting out the bucket and mop again. 'He can't help it.'

'I know,' said Mum.

'Poor darling Everton,' said Laura, and she went to boil him an egg, Everton's all-time favourite snack.

He ate it too. Every little bit.

'He really is getting better,' said Danny, lying down beside Everton and fondling his black and white ears.

Everton purred. He was still very stiff and sore, but he seemed happier in his new home now. He wouldn't try to escape again. Though they'd keep the windows shut to make sure.

'It's going to be all right, Everton, you'll see,' said Danny, and this time he was sure.

Jamila Gavin

PITCHOU

Raju was angry. He was so angry he thought he would burst.

'I hate Ma, I hate Pa, I hate Sonia.' Sonia was his elder sister. 'I hate my aunt and uncle and I hate the world.'

Raju's mother, father, and sister Sonia, had all gone to England to attend a wedding. Worse than that, instead of leaving him in Bombay, they packed him off to the country for two whole months of the summer holidays, to be with his boring aunt and uncle, who didn't even have children, and who lived in a boring little village miles from anywhere.

Raju's playground was Bombay – the streets and alleyways, the crowded old bazaars and the glittering new shopping arcades. When he got bored with that, he went to Crawford market, where great fat merchants sat on the tops of mountains of fruit and vegetables and sweets and spices and every possible kind of edible thing, yelling and shouting their wares. Or he went with his friends to the glitzy cinemas to see the latest films. If they had seen all the movies, there was always cricket on the *maidaan*, swimming in the sea or swaggering into the tearooms of international hotels to order milkshakes and lemonades.

Now here he was in a quiet rural village, where the loudest sound was the crowing of the cockerel and where most people went about on foot or in bullock carts.

The silence disturbed him. 'I hate it, I hate it, I hate it,' he stormed.

It was midday. Hardly anyone was about. Raju sulked around the garden with a stick in his hand, slashing at the bushes and hating with every muscle in his body. The hens and ducks who pecked and clucked softly as they pottered in the grass scuttled from beneath his stomping feet.

He felt mean. He wanted to bully something. He saw Queenie, his aunt's favourite shining black hen, all puffed out, half-hidden in the long grass under the lemon tree. He thrashed his stick at her. How pleased he felt, when she gave a pathetic squawk and heaved herself into the bushes.

That's when Raju saw the egg. He stared at it with faint surprise. He had only ever seen an egg in the market or in his mother's kitchen. What was an egg doing out here in the garden? He picked it up. It was warm, with bits of feathers stuck to it. He slowly realised that it must be Queenie's egg. She had been sitting on it, and he had chased her away. He felt a pang of guilt, but thought, 'Oh well, she's left it now, and finders keepers,' and he popped it in his pocket.

For a while, he just roamed around, looking at nothing in particular. His hand was in his pocket, cradling the egg. Its delicate, oval shape and extraordinary fragility, gave him an unexpected tremor of excitement. He forgot about feeling angry. He wondered if there was a chick inside it. He held it protectively, keeping it warm and safe.

That night, he cocooned the egg in straw and placed it under the warmth of his bedside light which he decided to leave on, and then went to sleep.

Tap, tap, tap, crick, crick, crick; it was only a small pipping sound, but persistent, and it piped its way into Raju's dream.

Tap, tap, tap, crick, crick, crick. Raju woke up. He looked at the egg beneath

his bedside lamp. It looked like a small planet, glowing in the black space of night all around. *Tap, tap, tap* ... the pipping sound got harder; then ... *CRACK*! The perfect, oval, white shell fractured.

Raju sat bolt upright in amazement. A little beak hammered away and burst through the shell. Then, before his very eyes, a dank, lank, scrawny little creature stepped out into the world as bold as brass, cheeping away for all it was worth.

For a moment, Raju was almost afraid. He had seen many strange and wonderful things in Bombay. He had seen snake-charmers draped in writhing pythons; monkeys who danced and turned cartwheels; he had seen magnificent elephants and camels and bears; he had even seen a tiger once, when he was taken to a jungle. But somehow he had never seen anything so magical as a simple white egg breaking open, and a living creature stepping out into the world.

Raju watched it with wonder. It was so small. Beneath the warmth of his bedside lamp, it shook itself and stretched its tiny wings. Soon, the wetness dried, and as it dried, the chick began to fluff up, all softly grey with yellow splodges.

Raju's hand closed over the creature and lifted it onto his palm.

He could feel its heart thudding inside its quivering body, and its dark eyes glistened like glass beads. He held it to his cheek. It was so soft. He looked at it again, standing in the palm of his hand, and it was as though he held creation itself.

He lay back on his pillow, holding the creature to his chest and fell asleep again.

The next morning at breakfast, his aunt and uncle looked at Raju with amazement. He had a smile on his face. They hadn't seen a smile since the day he came.

'You're looking mighty pleased with yourself today!' commented Uncle.

'Like the cat who got the cream,' agreed Aunt.

Then they heard a funny cheeping coming from somewhere. 'What's that?'

Raju reached into his shirt pocket and pulled out his little chick. 'I found this egg in the bushes yesterday. I kept it warm, first in my pocket then under my bedside lamp, and look – it hatched!' He proudly opened his hand and showed them the little grey chick, shaking and fluffing up its feathers and squawking for food.

'Well, I never did!' exclaimed Uncle with a laugh. 'You're a fine one, to be sure!' And Raju didn't know if his uncle meant him or the chicken.

'It must be one of Queenie's chicks,' exclaimed his aunt. 'How careless of her to leave it lying around!'

'I suppose I'd better give it back to its mother,' murmured Raju, guiltily remembering how he had frightened Queenie away.

'You can't do that, my boy!' cried Aunt. 'Queenie won't take this chick back. Not now that it's been in your pocket and in your hand. She won't recognise it any more. No, Raju, you hatched the chick. You're its mother now.'

Raju laughed. 'That's silly! Of course I'm not its mother.'

'The chicken thinks so. The chicken will think it looks like you because you were the first thing it saw when it hatched.

Raju popped the chicken onto the table in front of him and looked at it with amazement. The chicken gazed back with its beady eyes. Then it began cheeping hungrily, scratching with its pink, four-clawed feet and pecking at the breadcrumbs on the tablecloth.

Aunt poured some water into a saucer. 'Make sure it always has plenty to drink,' she said.

Instead of joining all the other chickens in the yard, the baby bird insisted on sticking as close to Raju as it could. Raju didn't mind. He gave his chicken a name – Pitchou – and spent hours cuddling it and chatting to it while he made sure it was fed and watered and looked after.

It pecked from his plate, and perched on the bath while he bathed, and slept on his bed and was carried round in Raju's shirt pocket wherever he went.

'One thing you should know, little chick,' Raju told it as he put it to bed one night, 'I'm not your mother, but I am your friend. Your very, very, best friend.'

It was amazing how fast the little chick grew. His soft, grey, downy feathers darkened and a bright red cockscomb began to grow on his head.

Soon Pitchou was too big to fit into Raju's pocket, so he rode on his shoulder or strutted after him on thin, peachy legs, never letting Raju out of his sight.

If Raju cycled down the long road to the bazaar, Pitchou came too, riding proudly in the front basket, his shiny head swivelling round as if he were the guide. If Raju rode on the bullock cart across the fields to the village, so did Pitchou. He even got into Uncle's car when they all went for a drive to visit friends.

Now that Raju had a friend, he became so much nicer. He smiled a lot, and didn't mind helping in the garden – feeding the hens and checking the hen sheds each day for eggs; and even though Pitchou sometimes got muddled up with all the other chickens, he always came running as soon as Raju called him.

Raju couldn't believe it when he realised that two months had passed. Suddenly it was time for him to go home. His bags were packed. Waiting patiently nearby was Pitchou. 'Wherever Raju goes, I go,' his puffed-up feathers announced.

Aunt and Uncle drove Raju to the bus station, and there they put him on the bus and made sure that all his luggage was safely tied on to the roof.

'What about that?' asked the bus driver, pointing at the chicken.

'That's my friend,' said Raju. 'He comes with me,' and he held Pitchou all the way back to Bombay.

Mum, Dad, and his sister Sonia were bursting to tell Raju all about their trip to England. But Raju was just as excited and told them all about Pitchou. Mother looked at Pitchou and said, 'You're not really keeping that chicken here, are you, Raju?'

'That's not just a chicken,' explained Raju. 'Pitchou thinks I'm his mother. He's got to stay with me.'

'But are you sure that a chicken will like living in a Bombay apartment, four floors up, rather than in a country garden?' murmured Father.

'Pitchou wants to be with me. He has never left my side since the day he hatched,' insisted Raju.

So Pitchou stayed. Somehow, though, it wasn't like Aunt's garden. Fluff and feathers and droppings were scattered all over the flat; when he fluttered around, he crashed into the television, or knocked over the ornaments, and messed all over the chairs and sofas; and he didn't seem to realise that the carpet wasn't the earth. He scraped and dug into it with his sharp claws just the same, tossing up shreds of wool; and he flew up into the curtains as if they were trees.

'It's no good,' sighed Mother finally. 'Either that chicken goes into the pot or back to the country.'

Raju looked at his mother as if she was a murderer. 'Into the pot? How could you even think of such a thing?' he howled. 'Eating my chicken would be like cannibalism!'

'Well then, it's back to the farm,' declared Mother. Father agreed. Raju held his beloved bird in his arms. 'But Pitchou thinks I'm his mother. He'll miss me. He'll be miserable.'

'Did you miss me all the time I was away?' demanded Raju's mother.

'Yes!' cried Raju. 'Well . . .' he added warily, 'not all the time. Only at first.'

'Well, then, it will be the same for Pitchou. 'He'll miss you at first, and then he'll adjust. After all, he's not a chick any more.' They all looked at the large, sleek, coal-black cock, with sharp, shining feathers and the arc of bright red cockscomb which glowed on his head. It's time he had friends of his own kind,' said Mother.

It was a miserable journey back to the country. Raju held his pet – his child – his friend – on his lap all the way back.

The only thing which comforted Raju was that his aunt and uncle promised that Pitchou would always be his.

'Do you promise not to eat him?' pleaded Raju.

'Of course we won't. Come here for your next holidays, and he'll be waiting for you.'

Sadly, Raju said goodbye. He could hardly bear to watch Pitchou's head bobbing frantically in a basket, as he tried desperately to follow him back to the car.

Another three months passed before Raju was able to return to the farm. The first thing he did was rush out in search of Pitchou.

'He's over in the big yard with the full-grown birds,' his aunt told him.

'Which one is Pitchou?' He looked and looked, calling out his name and holding out his hand as he always used to. But just when one bird came towards him, so did another and another.

'Which one is mine?' Raju asked his aunt despairingly.

'The one with a ring round its foot. I

knew it would soon be difficult to recognise him. We will let him live for ever, Raju, but I'm afraid chickens have very little brain, and not very good memories. Please don't be hurt that he doesn't remember you.'

Raju stood staring with disappointment. He strode in among the birds and grabbed Pitchou, who struggled and squawked and clawed his arm. But Raju held him firmly until he was quiet. He tried to look into his beady eyes, but there was no glimmer of recognition. He stroked his feathers sadly, then put him down. Pitchou paused just briefly, then scampered off to join the others as fast as his legs could carry him.

'How could you forget me so soon? After all, I am your mother!' sighed Raju. He walked down the length of the garden, carefully avoiding the hens and ducks who pecked and clucked in the sunshine. Deep in the shady, long grass beneath the lemon trees, he caught a glimpse of Queenie's shining black feathers. She sat perfectly still and didn't move as he drew near.

Raju smiled. Queenie was broody again. But this time, he wouldn't chase her away.

Chris Powling

THE GHOST GORILLA

A ghost gorilla . . .

Can you imagine such a thing? Huge and hairy, with sad gorilla eyes and rippling gorilla muscles, yet – at the same time – horribly, *horribly* invisible?

No, I couldn't believe it, either.

Actually, I was pretty sure it was a joke from the moment Darcy brought it to school. Darcy was that kind of kid. The trouble was, he *agreed* it was a joke straight away. 'That's a brilliant goldfish,' he said to my best friend Mel as he came up to us in the playground. 'And your stick insect is great, Sara! Got a name, has it?'

'Twiggy,' I told him.

'And this is Goldie,' said Mel.

Already we were goggle-eyed.

What grabbed our attention was the collar – the enormous, silver-studded collar – that Darcy was dangling in the air from the end of an old broomstick. Fixed to the front of the collar was a silver bell. It tinkled eerily as the collar swayed to and fro. 'What's that for, Darcy?' Mel asked.

Darcy looked up and bit his lip. 'That?' he said. 'Oh . . . nothing. Just a bit of a joke.'

'A joke?' I asked.

'Well . . . a *sort* of joke, Sara,' Darcy replied.

By now, of course, other kids had come over. Soon we were all gawping at the collar.

Darcy took no notice of this whatsoever. 'Is that your budgie,

Elroy?' he exclaimed. 'It's terrific! And I really like your gerbil, Nina. Daki's slow-worm is smashing, too. It's going to be really tough for Miss Westcott to choose which of them is best.'

'Best *looked-after*, Darcy,' I reminded him. 'That's what the project is all about.'

'Best looked-after, yes,' Darcy agreed. 'That's what I meant, Sara.'

Tinkle-tinkle-tinkle! went the silver bell.

Still everyone stared. And still Darcy took no notice. He was so busy admiring Josh's terrapins and Razia's white mice he seemed to have forgotten completely that he had a collar, big enough to fit a St Bernard, hanging from his broomstick like a weird, doggy halo.

Tinkle-tinkle-tinkle! the silver bell went.

Of course, by this time, no one wanted to notice it. What worried us was falling for one of Darcy's tricks – and then being teased about it for the rest of term. We'd all seen that happen, thank you. So we pretended to be fascinated by each other's pets, absolutely fascinated, as if the last thing in the world that interested us was Darcy and his floating dog-collar.

Eventually, it was a little kid who came to our rescue. 'Darcy,' he piped up.

'Is that a kite or what?'

'A kite?' said Darcy.

He looked all round for something kite-like till, as if by accident, he caught sight of the dog-collar. 'Oh, *that*,' he said. 'No, that's not a kite. That's my gorilla.'

'Gorilla?' the little kid blinked.

'The collar's round his neck,' Darcy told him. 'Don't worry, though. He isn't real. Actually, he's only a ghost gorilla.'

'A ghost gorilla!' gasped the little kid. He took a hasty step backwards.

To tell the truth, he wasn't the only one. What was so scary was the matter-of-fact way Darcy said it. It was as if the last thing he wanted to do was frighten us. 'He won't hurt you,' he promised. 'All he wants to do is haunt you – you know, give you the creeps an' such. Just like an ordinary ghost, really. Of course, he's a lot *stronger* than an ordinary ghost.'

'How do you know?' Razia asked.

'Know what?'

'How do you know he's stronger than an ordinary ghost – when you can't even see him?'

'Because he's a gorilla,' said Darcy. 'A gorilla is stronger than a person, yes? So a ghost-gorilla is bound to be stronger than a ghost-person. It stands to reason.'

'Yeah . . .' said Razia.

'Hold on,' I said. 'You told Mel and me that this is just one of your jokes, Darcy.'

'It is,' said Darcy.

'A joke, right?'

Darcy nodded quickly. 'Quite right, Sara. I admit it.'

Tinkle-tinkle-tinkle! went the silver bell.

It didn't seem like a joke. Darcy made sure of that by shifting his eyes warily over the space where the ghost gorilla was – would have been, I mean. Honestly, what a con-artist! 'Look,' I said, stepping forward. 'I'm waving my hands under the broomstick, see. There's nothing there.'

'True,' said Darcy.

'But you can walk *through* a ghost, Sara,' Mel pointed out.

'Or a ghost can walk through you,' Darcy added.

And, just above our heads, he traced a slow circle in the air with the silver-studded collar.

It was amazing.

For a split-second, I swear I heard the snort of hot gorilla breath on my cheek and the shuffle of massive gorilla feet almost stepping on mine. 'Only a joke,' said Darcy.

The little kid started to cry.

Luckily, that's when the bell rang. The school bell, that is, not Darcy's. As we scrambled into the classroom, though, I couldn't help seeing how Darcy hung back a bit, both hands round his broomstick, while kids who should have known better cleared a space all round him for the ghost gorilla. 'Just look at him,' I snarled. 'He's fooling the lot of them!'

'Yeah . . .' said Mel.

I glared at her in disgust. Was she fooled by Darcy, too? 'Miss Westcott will soon sort him out,' I predicted.

And so she did. 'A ghost gorilla?' she sniffed, when Darcy had explained. 'Are you ready to produce a handbook on how to look after him, Darcy? That's part of the project, too, you know.'

'Certainly, Miss,' said Darcy.

'Fine,' said Miss Westcott. 'I can't wait to see it, Darcy. Now, put your ghost gorilla in the stock cupboard, please. Under lock and key, I think. We don't want him to escape, do we?'

'Er . . . Miss,' Darcy said. 'He can walk *through* walls, you know. All ghosts can.'

'Not these walls, Darcy. These walls happen to be ghost-proof.'

'Ghost gorilla-proof as well, Miss?'

'Exactly, Darcy.'

Darcy sighed with relief. 'What a stroke of luck!' he said.

After this we settled down to our handbooks – at our desks, on the floor, behind the reading trolley, wherever we could find a space with our pets. Darcy worked by himself in the painting corner. This was strange, really, since it was about as far as he could get from the stock cupboard. Maybe he wanted to forget the ghost gorilla.

Maybe we all did.

But it wasn't easy. Somehow, in the

back of our minds, he was always there under lock and key – his knuckles brushing the games equipment on the floor, his head nudging the topmost shelf where we kept the science stuff.

Just before lunch, Miss Westcott came round for a final check on our progress. As usual, she left everyone beaming – everyone, that is, except Darcy. We all fell quiet when we picked up the sharpness in her voice. 'As a painting it's excellent, Darcy. I've never seen such a cloudy, steamy rainforest. I asked for a handbook, though – something that tells us how we should care for the creature we've chosen. There's no creature here at all.'

'It's too late, Miss,' said Darcy sadly. 'There's none of them left to see. *All* these gorillas are ghosts.'

'Ghosts?'

'Like the one I brought in this morning, Miss.' Casually, Darcy glanced across the room.

So did the rest of us.

Except we weren't nearly so casual. Mostly, our eyes were out on stalks. For above the sound of budgies and gerbils and white mice – not to mention a deafening roar here and there from the odd stick insect – we heard through the door of the stock cupboard, faintly but clearly, the ringing of a silver bell.

Tinkle-tinkle-tinkle!

It was Darcy's greatest trick. We all agreed about that even if we couldn't decide how he'd done it. My own theory is that he had help from Miss Westcott herself, who moved the project along to *Endangered Species* a little *too* smoothly in my opinion.

Pat Thomson

HAIR OF A CAT

At two o'clock in the morning the family were awakened by the most appalling screech. Ben, his heart racing, jumped out of bed and ran straight to his parents' room. He could hear Hannah crying and his mother was already hurrying across the landing to snatch her out of her cot. His father was also on his feet, standing at the top of the stairs. Ben saw him pause, look around for a weapon and seize the only available item. It was a large teddy bear. He grasped it purposefully by the leg. Ben knew it had a very hard head but he also knew the leg came off.

The noise was coming from the kitchen and was accompanied by the sound of breaking china and furniture falling. The family stood on the stairs, Dad carrying the bear, Ben behind him, holding up his pyjama trousers, and Mum bringing up the rear, with Hannah in her arms. Ben knew what Dad had to do now. He had to burst through the kitchen door, yelling 'Freeze!' but it didn't seem the same with a bear.

Dad made up his mind. He stepped forward opened the kitchen door – and groaned.

Peering round Dad's elbow, Ben looked into the room. Minette, their little black cat, was standing rigid on the draining board. Her tail was straight out and her fur reminded Ben of his experiments with iron filings. Broken crockery littered the floor, a chair had been overturned and

tomorrow's cornflakes spilled from the box all over the table. Crouched by Minette's food bowl was the cause of all the trouble. Ben stared straight into the unwinking marmalade eyes of the biggest ginger tom he had ever seen.

'I told you that cat flap was a mistake,' said Mum.

Minette took several days to get over it. She said as much to Roddy, the dog who lived next door.

'A monster! A great ginger monster! And it's been back.'

Roddy sighed. 'You don't know how to look after yourself, girl,' he said gruffly. 'You gotta face up to these bullies.'

'But it's enormous,' squeaked Minette. 'I get in the cupboard and keep quiet. I always leave a bit in my food bowl, though. I'd be afraid not to.'

'Well, here's where I've got good news for you. My lot are having a weekend in Derbyshire and they want your lot to look after me.'

'You mean you'll be staying the weekend? That would be a shock for the great beast.'

'Exactly,' said Roddy, smugly.

On Friday afternoon, Roddy's basket was brought round, his lead was hung behind the back door and several tins of dog food were stacked in the kitchen cupboard.

Minette had known Roddy since she was a kitten and felt safe with him. Not that he was a big dog. He was rather small. Postmen, however, treated him with respect and the milkman came early. The neighbour on the other side had called him 'a vicious little runt', but at the time there had been a coolness between him and Roddy's owner. She had bought a large mower and had been through his fence and half-way across his rhubarb before she found the 'off' switch.

Now, Roddy stalked the kitchen, sniffing experimentally and inspecting the cat flap.

'It's been here, all right,' he said. 'Pooh! Very nasty. We'll smell it coming. Now, let's place the troops. Minette, you get up on the draining board, and I'll station myself by the cat flap. Stay clear, unless, of course, you want to come down and nip it on the leg when I've got it down. Feel free.'

Roddy settled himself. He waited a long time. He had a good scratch, got up and stretched his legs and settled down again. He began to think of his basket. He wondered what Derbyshire was like. He wondered whether eight tins of dog food were enough for a weekend. What if they didn't come back for a week? Could he last on seven tins? Six tins? Five? Four? Three . . .

When Roddy jerked into wakefulness, it was because his nose was full of a ferocious odour of cat. It was so strong he felt faint. He opened his eyes on a ginger landscape. The cat was so near it blocked his view of the kitchen. It was looking at him. Roddy was mesmerised by the marmalade eyes. He struggled to his feet. The cat and he were the same size. His hair rose on his shoulders and he growled.

The cat simply growled back, and it was the most controlled, menacing growl Roddy had ever heard. He watched the cat's fur rising until the creature seemed twice as big. It was turning into a lion as he stared at it.

Then, without making any further noise, the cat silently raked Roddy's face with its claws, turned, and slid out of the cat flap.

Minette was very upset. She was angry with herself for sleeping, horrified by Roddy's scratches and puzzled by what had happened. There was no sign of a struggle and Roddy was very quiet. They retreated to the warm patch behind the garden shed and started all over again.

'We've got to get it tonight,' said Roddy. 'After that, you're on your own again.'

'But what can we do?' wailed Minette.

'No defeatist talk,' said Roddy, sharply. 'It's a monster, and that's the truth, but when you get a big bully, my girl, forget the muscle. Start using your brains.'

By the evening, they had made a

hundred plans, all useless. They ate their dinners in silence and both left a little food in their bowls.

'I'm still thinking,' Minette assured Roddy, 'but I'll do it from the draining board.' She leaped up, dislodging the washing-up mop which Ben had left in a bowl of water. Roddy happened to be standing right underneath.

'Thank *you*,' he snapped. 'My brain's all wet now. How can I think with a wet brain?'

'Sorry, Roddy.'

'No! Wait! That's it! Get down here, Minette. Help me with our water bowls. If I can get just one go at that ginger mug, I'll be satisfied . . .'

Ben was disturbed by a regular knocking noise. *Flap*! pause, *flap*! It was in the kitchen again. He padded downstairs and opened the door, quietly. Roddy was sitting by the back door with a washing-up mop in his mouth. As Ben watched, he dipped it

into one of the water bowls and waited. The cat flap swung open and the large ginger tom thrust its head in. Roddy smacked it hard with the dripping mop. The flap dropped as the big cat withdrew. It was angry but puzzled, and tried again. This time, Roddy caught it on the nose. It sneezed and jumped back, getting momentarily stuck. While it hissed and spat, Roddy took the opportunity to strike again. His weapon was clumsy but unpleasantly wet and the ginger monster didn't like it. It scrambled backwards in undignified haste and the flap fell. They heard the sound of its claws on the fence as it escaped into the next garden. Ben smiled sleepily and went back to bed.

The next morning, Ben tried to tell his mother what had happened, but the bowls were back in their places and the wet patches had dried. Roddy and Minette were curled up, sleeping late.

'Honestly, Mum! *Wham*! it went, *wham*! on the cat's nose!'

'Really, Ben, Roddy couldn't have worked out something like that. I expect you were dreaming.' She smiled to herself and swept over to the sink. Then, she paused and picked up the mop. Slowly, with finger and thumb, she picked off a long, ginger hair.